Songs for My Dog and Other Wry Rhymes

Max Fatchen is a journalist, poet and author who spends much of his time on an untidy, sunlit verandah of his home near Adelaide, eating biscuits and watching the world go by while Michael Atchison captures current affairs in his daily cartoons in the Adelaide *Advertiser*. They are, if one may use the well-worn words . . . good mates.

The poems in this book have been used in British and Australian festivals, recited in major speech and drama competitions, appeared frequently on the BBC and in its publications and also on commercial television and radio and in mini-series.

Also by Max Fatchen

Just Fancy, Mr Fatchen
Forever Fatchen
Mostly Max

CHILDREN'S FICTION
The River Kings
Conquest of the River
The Spirit Wind
Chase Through the Night
The Time Wave
Closer to the Stars
Had Yer Jabs?

VERSE
Songs for My Dog and Other People
Wry Rhymes for Troublesome Times
A Paddock of Poems
A Pocketful of Rhymes
A Country Christmas
Tea for Three (with Colin Thiele)
Peculiar Rhymes and Lunatic Lines

Songs for My Dog

and Other Wry Rhymes

MAX FATCHEN

Illustrated by Michael Atchison

Wakefield Press

Wakefield Press
17 Rundle Street
Kent Town
South Australia 5067

Songs for My Dog first published by Kestrel Books 1980
Published by Puffin Books 1982
Wry Rhymes for Troublesome Times first published by Kestrel Books 1983
Published by Puffin Books 1985

Typeset by Clinton Ellicott, Wakefield Press
Printed and bound by Hyde Park Press, Adelaide

National Library of Australia
Cataloguing-in-publication entry

Fatchen, Max, 1920– .
Songs for my dog and other wry rhymes.
Rev. ed.

ISBN 1 86254 478 6.

I. Title

A821.3

For Claire, Sarah, Jonathan, Dominic,
Nicholas, Jessica and Butterfly, the poodle

CONTENTS

FOREWORD

These poems, since their first publication by Kestrel in the 1980s, have found their way into more than 120 anthologies throughout the English-speaking world. They all began with a small white poodle called Butterfly, who took the author's lumbering form on night walks in the outer Adelaide suburb of Smithfield. I wrote a poem for Butterfly but then poesy claimed my pen and, more properly, my old typewriter, and we were off into a world of raddled riddles and romping rhymes about almost anything that would interest children and make adults feel young again. I was lucky to find an illustrator of the skill and humour of Michael Atchison, who is also a dog person and whose small, talkative dog accompanies him in his daily cartoons in the Adelaide *Advertiser*. So this book is to remind us that the child lurks in us always and I hope it brings fun and entertainment for children and encourages them to write too – but especially to know that fun is alive and well, and that children themselves are terribly important and precious to writers and to all humankind.

Max Fatchen
Smithfield, 1999

Dogs and Cats and Budgerigars

THE COUNTRY DOG

The country dog with his eager grin
Enjoys the sound of the market din.
    To a city dog, he's a noisy clown,
      He likes a scrap when he comes to town.

The rushing road and the traffic's beat
He sits up straight in the wide front seat.
    He likes the seat of a country car
      His head stuck out where the breezes are.

He likes the run of the open land
Where the creekbeds wind and the big trees stand.
By the shining dam with its local frog,
With one ear cocked, goes the country dog.

By tractor seat or the furrow's line
He'll sit and wait for his master's sign.
With tireless paw and a bark or yelp
He runs the farm with the farmer's help.

There's a paddock lunch with the watching crows
But the country dog each wise bird knows.
The hours will dustily drift away
And there comes an end to a dog's long day.

The restless sheep on the ranges cry
The weary wind for the dawn will sigh
The small flames drowse on the old bush log
And light the dreams of the country dog.

CATNAP

My cat sleeps
with her claws
clasped
and her long tail
curled.
My cat twitches
her tabby cheek
for the mice that
squeak
and the milk that
flows
by her pink, pink nose
in the purring warmth
of my cat's world.

SAD TALE OF A WORDY BIRD

Septimus Smitherby sat on his perch
    And talked to a wondering throng.
He outdid the parson who preached at the church,
    His words indescribably long.

A budgerigar who was making his mark –
    Professors were spellbound to hear
His learned discussions. They'd cry 'Hush' and 'Hark'
    Or wear cottonwool in each ear.

But this chattering bird grew too big for his beak
    Consider how sorry his plight is.
He's no longer the rage. Printed large on his cage
    Is a notice which says 'Laryngitis'.

NIGHT WALK

What are you doing away up there
On your great long legs in the lonely air?
    Come down here, where the scents are sweet,
    Swirling around your great, wide feet.

How can you know of the urgent grass
And the whiff of the wind that will whisper and pass
    Or the lure of the dark of the garden hedge
    Or the trail of a cat on the road's black edge?

What are you doing away up there
On your great long legs in the lonely air?
    You miss so much at your great, great height
    When the ground is full of the smells of night.

Hurry then, quickly, and slacken my lead
For the mysteries speak and the messages speed
    With the talking stick and the stone's slow mirth
    That four feet find on the secret earth.

So Big!

The dinosaur, an ancient beast,
I'm told, was very large.
His eyes were big as billiard balls,
His stomach, a garage.
He had a huge and humping back,
A neck as long as Friday.
I'm glad he lived so long ago
And didn't live in my day!

There was a young fellow called Hugh
Who went to a neighbouring zoo.
    The lion opened wide
    And said, 'Come inside
And bring all your family too.'

Raddled Riddles

Why did the beetroot blush? They say
It saw the salad dressing.
'O have a heart,' the cabbage said,
'I haven't finished guessing.'

Why did the chicken cross the road?
To reach the other side.
I wish she hadn't gone, that's all,
She's now most crisply fried.

Me ...

GROWING

When I grow up I'll be so kind,
Not yelling 'Now' or 'Do you MIND!'
    Or making what is called a scene,
    Like 'So you're back' or 'Where've you BEEN?'
Or 'Goodness, child, what is it NOW?'
Or saying 'STOP ... that awful row',
    Or 'There's a time and place to eat'
    And 'Wipe your nose' or 'Wipe your feet'.
I'll just let people go their way
And have an extra hour for play.
    No angry shouting 'NOW what's wrong?'
    It's just that growing takes so long.

HAIR

I despair
About hair
    With all the fuss
    For us
Of snipping
And clipping,
    Of curling
    And twirling,
Of tying
And drying,
    And lopping
    And flopping,
And flurries
And worries,
    About strength,
    The length,
As it nears
The ears
    Or shoulder.
    When you're older
It turns grey
Or goes away
    Or leaves a fuzz
    Hair does!

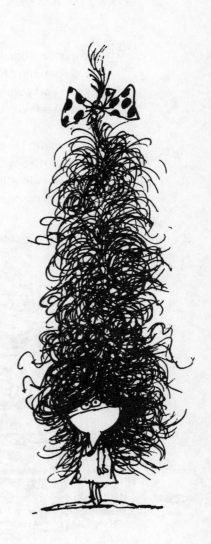

ANYONE SEEN MY ...

The people who keep losing things
    Are searching high and low.
They poke and peer – 'We left it here.'
    But no one seems to know.

The people who keep losing things
    Have not a single clue.
They look in vain – 'It's lost, *again*.
    I can't just wear *one* shoe.'

For people who keep losing things
    There isn't any cure.
They carry on – 'It *can't* be gone.
    I left it there, I'm *sure*.'

They wear a look of great surprise
    To think that it's mislaid.
A sock, a vest and all the rest,
    Are stolen, lost or strayed.

The people who keep losing things –
    They worry and they whine.
They can't think where … but, most unfair,
    They go and borrow mine.

NOT IN BED YET!

Getting Albert off to bed
    Is such an anxious task,
He never seems to want to go
    Although you ask
And ask.

'Just five more minutes,' Albert says.
    Another five, and then
Before you know it, cunning boy,
    He stretches it
To ten.

He brushes teeth with lazy strokes
    He lingers and he plays.
'Please HURRY, Albert,' people shout
    But Albert stays
And stays.

Getting Albert into bed
    Would seem a losing fight.
I think I'll go to bed
Instead.
So, everyone,
    Goodnight!

A football fanatic in strife
Found telly had altered his life.
    Now his eyes are quite square
    With a switch in his hair
And he's turned on and off by his wife.

On this subject I'm sorry to speak
It happened on Saturday week.
   They loaded poor Gran
   In a furniture van
And auctioned her off as antique.

WHEN I'M READY ...

Doing things immediately,
    When they scold.
Doing things straight away,
    When I'm told.
Doing things at once
    Or there'll be a row,
And being told
    FOR THE LAST TIME
To do it now,
    Only makes me fidget
And frown,
And slow right down,
Until ...
And you can bet,
    An hour later
I haven't done it yet.

KNOW-ALLS

I hate know-alls
And show-alls.
    I get wild
When people say,
    'Look, child!'
And nag
And finger-wag.
I'd like a gag
Or a bag
    To put over their heads,
    Especially,
When all along,
I *know* jolly well,
They're wrong!

WHO'S SCARED NOW?

I'm warning you.
Don't scare me.
Don't go 'Boo'.
Will you?
Don't say you're from space
Or some awful place.
That you're a deep-sea creature
Or a late-night movie monster,
Will you?
Because –
ZAP!
POW!
I'm disintegrating you now.
Click,
Tick!
You are reassembled
And changed,
Your matter
Rearranged,
Thirteen million light years away,
If it's a day,
On the planet Zen,
With a scratchy pen,
Doing four million lines,
In the Homework Mines.
And it serves you right
For frightening me last night.

Nutty Nursery Rhymes

'Jump over the moon?' the cow declared,
   'With a dish and a spoon. Not me.
I need a suit and a rocket ship
   And filmed by the BBC.

'I want a roomy capsule stall
    For when I blast away,
And an astronaut as a dairymaid
    And a bale of meadow hay.'

She gave a twitch of her lazy rump,
    'Space travel takes up time.
I certainly don't intend to jump
    For a mad old nursery rhyme.'

There was a young woman called June
Whose mealtime was midnight to noon,
    And after she ate
    She demolished the plate
And swallowed the knife, fork and spoon.

Little Jack Horner hasn't his plum,
    We're keeping the fact rather quiet.
He's putting on weight and it worries his Mum
    So he's now on a pie-free diet.

Simple Simon met a pieman
On a fairground trip.
Two happy souls, with sausage rolls
They're now in partnership.

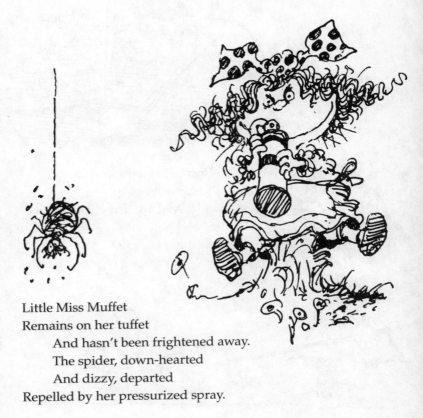

Little Miss Muffet
Remains on her tuffet
And hasn't been frightened away.
The spider, down-hearted
And dizzy, departed
Repelled by her pressurized spray.

Humpty Dumpty didn't dare fall
When his wife bought carpet wall-to-wall.

Don't mention sheep
To Little Bo-peep
    And all their stupid habits.
She's home these days
And full of praise
    For guinea pigs and rabbits.

Jack and Jill
Are with us still
 No tumble or mishap.
A hill to scale?
Oh fetch the pail
 And use the kitchen tap.

Rockabye baby
 On the stairtop,
Crying and screaming
 When will she stop?
Is it her temper?
 The way that she's pinned?
Rockabye baby
 It's simply the wind.

Fish Fingers

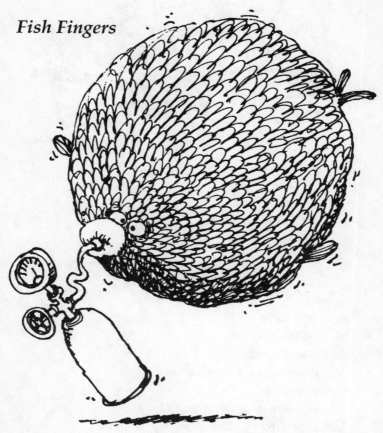

A puffer fish blows up with air
    And some may think this crafty.
It blows and blows,
And so it grows,
    But goodness me, how draughty.

While crabs may have their little cares
   And doubt that sometimes gnaws,
They *do* believe in love and friends
   And also, Santa Claws.

If you hold a shell to your ear, they say,
   You'll hear the sea winds blow.
I held one to my ear. It said:
   ''Ullo, 'ullo, 'ullo.'

Squid squirt ink
    When alarmed,
But I'm inclined to think
    If they're unharmed
And taking their ease
    In the seas,
They'll write to their mothers
    And brothers,
Whom they love dearly,
    Using their ink instead
    To ask 'How's Fred?'
And signing,
    'Yours sincerely'.

I wonder at the jellyfish
That like to drift and drowse
And seem to wear without a care
A kind of see-through blouse.

A fish had remarked to a chip,
'Unless we can give them the slip,
When the fat starts to fry
I'm afraid it's goodbye
And it won't be a very nice trip.'

A hungry shark some bathers eyed,
His wife said in the spray,
'How would you like your food, my dear,
Eat here or takeaway?'

Improbable Tails

THE PORPOISE'S TAIL

'Will you walk a little faster,' said the whiting to the snail,
'There's a porpoise close behind me and he's treading
    on my tail.'

Lewis Carroll

'A whiting's tail is tiny,
    A whiting's very small.'
That's what a porpoise told me,
    'It wasn't us at all.'

The porpoise said respectfully,
    'It's really such a shame
That such a grumpy little fish
    Can spoil the porpoise name.

'I'm not the one to quarrel,'
    It pondered in the tide,
'But really, in this story,
    You've only heard one side.'

Its eyes were bright and salty
    With such a friendly snout,
'It's not the things the whiting says
    But those that it leaves out.

'For when we leap and frolic
    Within the seven seas,
The motto of a porpoise
    Is "Mind Your Manners, Please".

'We *always* murmur "pardon"
    Or even "after you".'
How could I doubt a porpoise
    So honest and true blue?

So when I eat a whiting
    And crack its tiny ribs,
I smack my lips and whisper,
    'Take *that* for telling fibs.'

JACK'S THE BOY

*And when they awoke, the beanstalk had grown like
an enormous tree, disappearing into the sky ...*

Clamber up the beanstalk, Jack,
To where the white clouds drift.
    Jack stands and smirks.
    He slyly lurks,
He's waiting for the lift.

WELL LAID

The goose that lays the golden egg
Avoids the thief and fox.
   With cackling din,
   She's laid it in
Her safe deposit box.

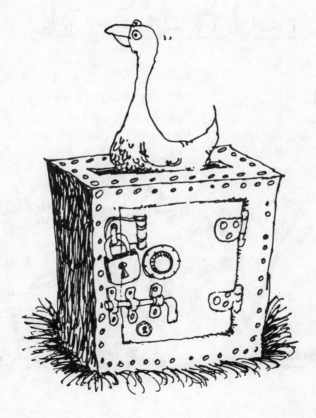

Horrible Happenings

My dog is such a gentle soul,
Although he's big it's true.
He brings the paper in his mouth.
He brings the postman too.

When Aunt Louisa lit the gas
    She had the queerest feeling.
Instead of leaving by the door
    She vanished through the ceiling.

Now here's a thought to ponder,
    Please try to understand.
Don't pat a boa-constrictor,
    He'll squeeze more than your hand.

I don't wish to harp about Lew
Who kept peering into the stew.
 He lifted the lid
 And in it he slid.
I think I'll miss dinner, don't you?

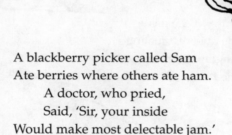

A blackberry picker called Sam
Ate berries where others ate ham.
 A doctor, who pried,
 Said, 'Sir, your inside
Would make most delectable jam.'

Little John was not content
Unless he played with wet cement.
 One day, alas, in someone's yard,
 He stayed too long and set quite hard.
His mother didn't want him home
So now he's just a garden gnome.

An uncle with wrinkles and creases
Detested his nephews and nieces.
    He said, 'I prefer
    When they come down and stir
To slice them in very small pieces.'

A young baby-sitter respected
By parents was sternly ejected.
    On a baby she sat
    Until it was flat
Which wasn't quite what they expected.

Erica, Miranda and Barrington Brown

OH ERICA, NOT AGAIN!

Every time we go on the pier,
    Or down to the sea, that is,
Erica says she is feeling queer
    And it makes her poor head whizz.

Erica says she likes the land,
    And there isn't, alas, much doubt,
As soon as she steps on a trippers' boat
    Erica's legs give out.

Erica's hands will clutch the rail.
    She hears the timbers creak.
She wonders where the lifebelts are –
    Or if we've sprung a leak.

There's never a sign of storm or gale
    But mother's crying 'Quick!'
And so it's just the same old tale,
    Erica's sick!

DON'T GO, MIRANDA

Here comes Miranda with riddles and jokes.
  Here comes Miranda again,
With a bagful of sweets and a couple of cokes
  To show her superior brain.

Miranda asks questions that certainly drag.
  She puts us to shame when at school.
But she's bringing the cokes and a jellybean bag
  So we're playing it friendly and cool.

The answers to riddles we simply don't know
  For somehow our brain-box grows numb.
We try very hard not to tell her to go
  When she's calling us 'stupid' and 'dumb'.

Miranda's a know-all and gives herself airs.
    She's terribly old in her ways.
But she's buying us chips and some chocolate eclairs,
    So isn't it better she stays?

BE QUIET!

The world's greatest snorer
  Was Barrington Brown.
His snores shook the windows
  And rattled the town.

The people grew frantic
  And fearful with fright,
And cried to each other,
  'What happens tonight?'

They lullabyed softly
  But who could ignore
The deafening noise
  Of that terrible snore?

They tied up their heads
  And their eardrums they bound,
But nothing could soften
  That thundering sound.

They made a giant clothes-peg
 And placed on his nose.
With one mighty snore
 Like a rocket it rose.

So they all left the town
 In their cars and their carts,
'We must be away
 Before Barrington starts.'

Then Barrington woke,
 'Where's everyone gone?'
And then he turned over
 And went snoring on!

Why Is It?

Why is it,
That,
In our bathroom,
It's not the dirtiest
Or the strongest
Who stay longest?
BUT
It always seems to be
The one who gets there
Just ahead
Of me.

Why is it
That people fret
When they're wet,
With loud cries
And soap in their eyes
And agonized howls,
Because they forget
Their towels?

Why is it that –
When *I'm* in the bath,
Steaming and dreaming,
My toes just showing
And the hot water flowing,
That other people
Yell and say,
'Are you there to stay
Or just on a visit?'

Why is it?

Look Out!

TIME PIECES

What makes a clock so slovenly
    And such a sad disgrace?
Because it doesn't wash its hands
    Or even clean its face.
What makes a clock bad-mannered
    And full of dongs and din?
It's when you try to hush it up
    It keeps on chiming in.

LOOK OUT!

The witches mumble horrid chants,
You're scolded by five thousand aunts,
    A Martian pulls a fearsome face
    And hurls you into Outer Space,
You're tied in front of whistling trains,
A tomahawk has sliced your brains,
    The tigers snarl, the giants roar,
    You're sat on by a dinosaur.
In vain you're shouting 'Help' and 'Stop',
The walls are spinning like a top,
    The earth is melting in the sun
    And all the horror's just begun.
And, oh, the screams, the thumping hearts –
That awful night before school starts.

BE NICE TO RHUBARB

Please say a word for rhubarb,
    It hasn't many chums
For people like banana splits
    Or fancy juicy plums.

They slice the sweet, sweet melon
    Or gather tasty pears,
But if you mention rhubarb pie
    You get the *rhu*dest stares.

They praise the yellow lemon,
    The golden orange cool,
But rhubarb's never mentioned
    – Or that's the general *rhu*le.

For rhubarb stewed and blushing
    I've only this to say,
If they should cast an unkind barb
    I'll see they *rhu* the day.

THAT'S THE TRUTH

When you are young,
    And dimply,
    You'll simply
    Go pimply.
That's the truth.
It's youth,
    Older people say;
    But they,
With their smirks
    And grins,
    Get extra chins.
Which is fair.
So there!

Australian Windmill Song

By the clay-red creek on the dry summer day,
 With never a trickle or pool,
An old windmill stands with a racketing wheel
 And it sings of the water that's cool.

And the sheep hear its song on the long, dusty plains
 While the rusty tank leaks at its seams
And the old windmill sings of the far-away rains
 And the grass of the sheep farmer's dreams.

The scummy trough stands where the thirsty sheep come
 And the magpies and crows dip their beaks,
While the wind on the wheel with its summer breath drums
 And the whirlwinds will dance past the creeks.

But the old windmill goes with a wheeze and a clank
 With the sun beating down on its tower
As it lifts up the water to flow in the tank
 While the sheep farmer longs for a shower.

The night's full of stars and the moon's bright and low
    And it climbs from the ranges nearby
And the soft-muzzled 'roos to the water trough go
    By the tank that must never run dry.

The farmer will smile at the racket and thump,
    Then he sleeps for he's lulled by the sound
As the windmill draws life with the pulse of its pump
From the sweet, hidden streams underground.

There was a pop singer called Fred
Who sang through the top of his head.
   It came as a blow
   When the notes were too low
So he sang through his toenails instead.

SPACE SPOT

Twinkle, twinkle little star
    Up there in the blue.
How I wonder what you are,
    Are you Dr Who?

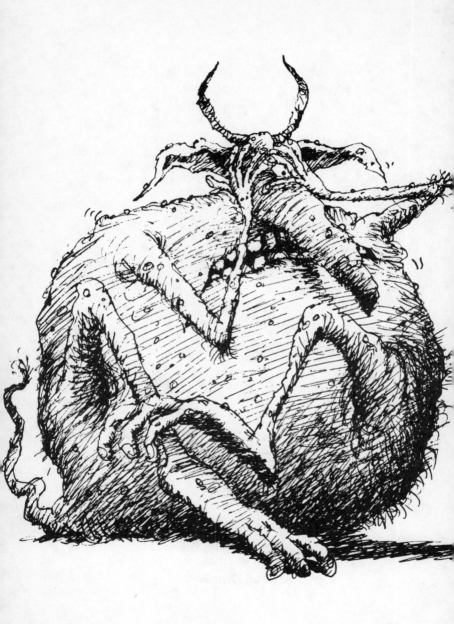

I often meet a monster
While deep in sleep at night;
And I confess to some distress.
It gives me quite a fright.
But then again I wonder.
I have this thought, you see.
Do little sleeping monsters scream
Who dream
Of meeting me?

Windowsills and Railway Thrills

WINDOWSILLS

A windowsill seems a nice spot to sit
For a box of bright flowers or a sparrow,
But for children who want to relax for a bit
They make them a little too narrow.

You can lean on a windowsill, looking outside,
With your hands propping under your chin
To a world that is rolling, both restless and wide
From the warm little world that you're in.

The windowsill gathers the dust, but again
There's someone who's keeping it clean.
You can coat it with varnish (so people explain)
Or paint it a pot-planty green.

I think that the man who invented them said,
'The sill of the window? Oh that.
It's a simple idea that I had in my head
As a place for my sun-loving cat.'

Orbit an Aunt

Some day
I wish that Aunty May
Could join the race
As the first aunt
Into Space.
It would save her peering
And interfering,
Lifting saucepan lids
And chastising kids.

Then, instead,
I could point overhead,
'LOOK! ...
Just left of the Milky Way,
That's Aunty May.'

The Railway Historical Steam Weekend

'Will you come,' says the letter, 'and join our outing.
Meal provided and time to spend
Along a line that is rarely travelled
For the railway historical steam weekend.'

The guard is dressed in his railway splendour,
With buttons and braid in a beautiful blend.
The engine's green, with a shining tender
For the railway historical steam weekend.

We stare at the signals old and ailing,
Our carriages labelled with their class.
The luggage rack has a real brass railing
And larks awake in the railyard grass.

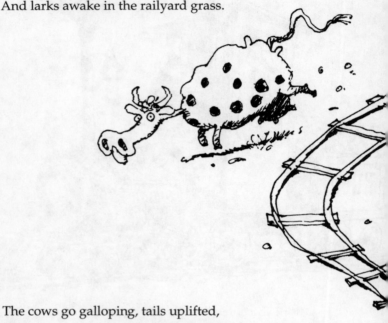

The cows go galloping, tails uplifted,
The carriages sway with a rackety beat.
A banner of smoke on the fields has drifted.
It's my turn now for the window seat.

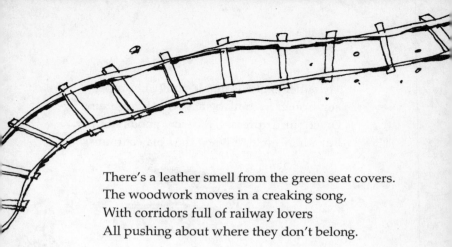

There's a leather smell from the green seat covers.
The woodwork moves in a creaking song,
With corridors full of railway lovers
All pushing about where they don't belong.

My father's loaded with information
On regulations and rules and Acts
And pages and pages on varying gauges
And funnels and tunnels and railway facts.

My father explains that it's quite improper
For mother to think he has wheels for brains
Describing expresses, the slow goods stopper,
But adults go mad when they play at trains.

So he looks at his watch as our time grows shorter,
Announcing the stations along our run.
He's wearing a cap with the title 'Porter'
For he likes to join in the railway fun.

We huff through cuttings with old rockfaces
And clatter on bridges above slow creeks
To all the mysterious railway places,
With a coal-black smudge on our wind-whipped cheeks.

We visit the engine at one small siding,
It hisses and pants like an iron god.
The driver is peering and prodding at pistons
And poking the great connecting rod.

Then on again with the white steam spouting
While signals dip near the journey's end.
My father says what a splendid outing,
A most educational steam weekend …

Well-organised and a worthwhile function,
With smoky wind and the rocking bend.
(But I liked tea at the local junction
On the railway historical steam weekend.)

Ruinous Rhymes

Pussycat, pussycat, where have you been,
Licking your lips with your whiskers so clean?
Pussycat, pussycat, purring and pudgy,
Pussycat, pussycat. WHERE IS OUR BUDGIE?

This little pig went to market
But I think that the point is well taken –
It's the cute little pig that wisely stayed home
Who succeeded in saving his bacon.

Mary, Mary, quite contrary,
How does your garden grow?
With snails and frogs and neighbours' dogs
And terribly, terribly slow.

Sing a song of sixpence?
It's hardly worth the sound.
So if you want my singing
Please offer me a pound.

When Old Mother Hubbard
Went to the cupboard
Her dog for a morsel would beg.
'Not a scrap can be found,'
She explained to her hound
So he bit the poor dear on the leg.

Proceed With Care: Parents Ahead

'WE WON'T TELL YOU AGAIN!'

It makes me sullen and wilful and wild
The way I'm described as a difficult child.
They shake their heads wherever I go
And tell each other, 'I told you so.'
They tell each other and even a friend,
'We don't quite know where it all will end.'
And tale on tale they have mournfully piled
On the life they lead with a difficult child.

But when I'm sweet and I smile and purr,
They say to each other, 'Now what's with her?'
And when I'm cuddly and kind and warm,
They say it's the calm before the storm.
And when I offer a hug or kiss
They're murmuring, 'What are you up to, Miss?'

JUST FANCY THAT

'Just fancy that!' my parents say
At anything I mention.
They always seem so far away
And never pay attention.

'Just fancy that,' their eyes are glazed.
It grows so very wearing.
'Just fancy that' is not a line
For which I'm really caring.

And so today I'm telling them
I threw a cricket bat.
I broke a windowpane at school.
They murmur, 'Fancy that.'

I wrote a message on the fence.
I spoke a wicked word.
The way the vicar hurried past,
I'm positive he heard.

'Just fancy that.' Then suddenly
Their eyes are sticking out,
Their words are coming in a rush
Their voices in a shout.

'You naughty child, you shameless boy,
It's time WE had a chat.'
Hurrah, they've noticed me at last.
My goodness, fancy that!

So Forgetful!

My father's memory is absolutely unique,
He can remember footballers, horses
And what won last week.
He knows about fishing bait,
The economy's state,
When to post his Pools
And what's wrong with schools.
His figures are never-ending
About Government spending;
But isn't it funny?
And I'll be perfectly frank,
When it comes to remembering my pocket-money,
His mind goes blank.

'Your room is like a pigsty,'
Say some in tones of doom;
But older pigs scold younger pigs,
'Your pigsty's like a room.'

A SHORT, SUMMERY THIN, THONG SONG

The song
of a
thong
is a
flip,
flap,
flong
that echoes
wherever
you go.
There aren't
any places
for silly
old laces
but a thing
that holds
on to
your toe.

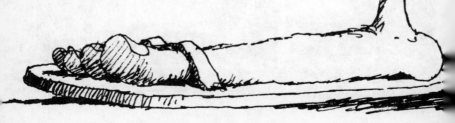

You're flapping
and tapping
with feet
overlapping
and people who watch
will agree
that the song
of a thong
when you're
flopping along
is of feet
that are born
to be
free.

Crafty Creatures

The flea is small
And no one's pet
But likes to hear
Of Dogs to Let.

There's nothing new about the gnu
That I could tell you here.
When young gnus play,
Tired mothers say,
'Don't be a *gnu*sance, dear.'

A waiting tortoise, looking cross,
Was answered by his mate.
'I missed the bus
But why the fuss,
I'm only six months late.'

The ravenous snail
Makes a long, shining trail
While clad in the slimiest garb,
If it's feeling unwell
It retires to its shell
For a nap and a dose of bicarb.

Guinea-pigs proliferate
At a most alarming rate;
So you'd better heed a warning.
Have you counted them this morning?

BEWARE

This cunning creature in its lair,
You'll find, is lurking everywhere.
There may be one (or even two).
It could be sitting next to you.
With staring eyes it's on the prowl.
It gives a sudden roar (or howl)
And, in a flash, to your dismay
It's leaping forward to its prey.
Beware each night this fearful danger –
The dreaded telly channel changer.

Slow Down For Boys

OH, BROTHER!

My brother's a motorbike freak.
Each week,
He rides races
In the oddest places.
He climbs hills,
Has spills.
He speeds
And cruises.
He gets action,
Satisfaction,
But mostly,
He gets bruises.

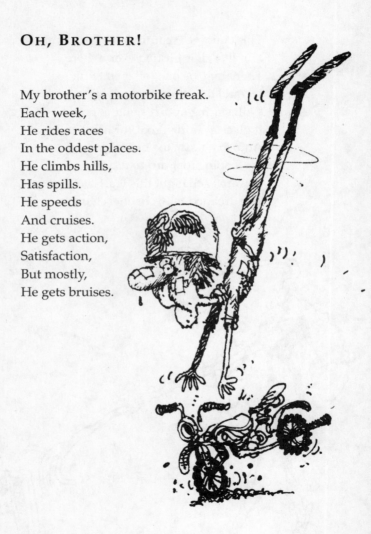

CONTROL CALLING

Just when I am conducting
A manoeuvre tactical
On my spaceship galactical,
Using my unidentified-object locators,
With my forward disintegrators
Whamming and shooting,
And my astro-clad officers saluting
Amid the rocketry's swirls and swishes,
My sister Kate
Cries 'Activate'
And I'm back on earth,
Drying dishes.

NOTHING, THAT'S WHAT

'What ARE you doing, Rupert?'
There comes the same reply,
For Rupert answers, 'Nothing.'
And that's his daily cry.

'What are you DOING, Rupert?
Who broke the garden pot?'
But Rupert answers, 'Nothing.'
And nothing's not a lot.

Whenever people blame him
For doing such-and-such
Then Rupert's doing nothing,
Which isn't very much.

'We want to SEE you, Rupert,
Who made this awful mess?'
But Rupert's doing nothing.
Well, nothing more or less.

And so we have this problem
To puzzle anyone,
How Rupert's doing nothing,
Yet naughty things get done.

Little Jim at last is clean.
They put him in the wash-machine.
He spun and dried without a sound.
Now there's a boy who's been around.

RANDOM ROT

'Children should be seen not heard.'
May I add a weary word?
Baby Bruce whose teeth aren't right
Loud and clear, is heard all night.

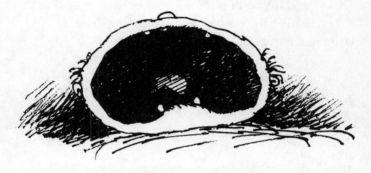

If they can muffle motorcars
Then why not noiseless cookie-jars?

Wings and Things

DINNER IS SERVED

When our almonds are ripe in the wind-shaken trees
And I'm thinking of one I might choose,
Then in from the ranges, with screeching delight
Comes a party of white cockatoos.

I don't recall sending a dinner-time card
Or asking them into my tree,
Or dropping the poor little shells in my yard
In the midst of their cockatoo tea.

What, dressing for dinner? Well yes, in a way
They're dressed in their cockatoo best,
Their snowy white plumage they nicely display,
With a bright yellow tinge on their crest.

They sit on the branches and hold in their claws
The almonds I've hoarded for weeks;
And they eat them with pleasure and never a pause
With a crack of their business-like beaks.

Almond cake I had planned for a party one night,
Almond toffee of rich, golden hues,
Alas with my plans they have all taken flight
Inside of those white cockatoos.

INSIDE STORY

A wonderful bird is the pelican,
His bill will hold more than his belican.

A pelican, who heard this verse,
Remarked to me, 'Good gracious,
I know my stomach and my bill
Are what you'd call capacious

'And yet a reputation that
For food and fish I scrimmage
Will mark me as a greedy bird
And somewhat spoil my image.

'I do admit, well now and then,
Inside my bill I'm popping
Unwary fish, but then again
It's handy too for shopping.

'And so before I leave I must
In case I'm thought neglectful
Explain it so you'll be, I trust,
A little more respectful.

The great advantage of a bill
Which cannot be denied,
Is simply opening it to fill
The roomy space inside.

'So any morsel, straying past,
Could finish in this catchment
And that is why my bill and I
Have such a strong attachment.'

I humbly thanked this pompous bird.
I've now a different slant
On what a pelican can do
And what a pelican't.

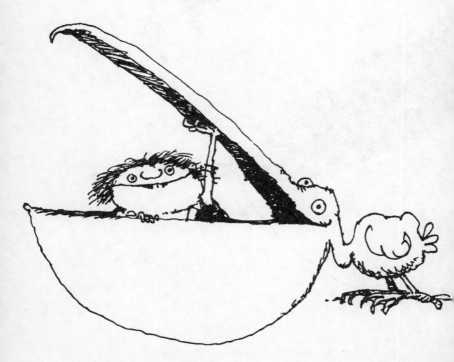

If pigs flew
And birds grunted
The world would seem
All back-to-fronted.

Poor Doris, so terribly tender
Was somehow caught up in a blender.
It beat her to pulp
And well you might gulp.
The chances are slim that they'll mend her.

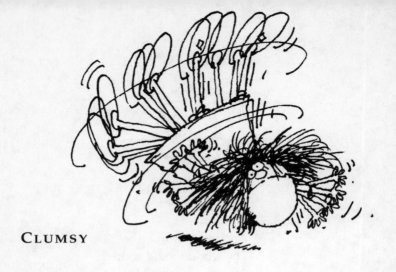

CLUMSY

My sister
 trips
   over any old thing
    while giving
     the loudest
      of squeals;
       over shoes,
        over mats,
         over chairs,
          over cats
           and finally
            head over heels.

Briny Bits

The boy stood on the burning deck,
A braver lad than most,
And said: 'It's rather warm for feet
But wonderful for toast.'

There occurred a most terrible scene
When a ship of the Merchant Marine
Lost a cargo of soap
At the Cape of Good Hope
And none of the crew would come clean.

Said a whale to her daughter whose spouting
Brought sailormen pointing and shouting,
'When they cry "Thar she blows"
Please attend to your nose
Or this is the end of your outing.'

Mermaids no longer croon the songs
That sailors found rewarding
For now they rock around the dock
And play a tape-recording.

ROWBOATS

I like rowboats, little rowboats,
Where you dip the oars and glide,
Listening to the seagull chatter
And the talking of the tide.

Sister Betty's at the tiller.
She has volunteered to steer.
Shep, the dog, is barking for'ard,
Keeping other vessels clear.

I'm the captain, giving orders,
Writing entries in the log,
Ready for repelling boarders,
Who will dare an old sea-dog?

Now we're Vikings from the Northland,
Taking longboats through the spray,
Writing in my longboat logbook,
'Sacked another town today.'

Was there ever such an ocean,
Spouting whales and Pirate Jack?
Sister Betty's suncream lotion
Oozes down her speckled back.

Gently on the wavelets pitching,
Listening to the sea's old sound,
Betty moans her nose is itching.
'LOOK OUT, BETTY! WE'RE AGROUND.'

Arms and legs and oars all flailing.
Words that make the paintwork blister.
When the seven seas you're sailing,
NEVER take a sunburnt sister!

Relax and Play, or Blow Away

IT'S A BIT RICH

Playing Monopoly's
Really my scene.
I hang on to houses
And play very mean.

I take all the money.
There's often a stack.
I'm not very pleasant
When giving it back.

I'm harsh as a landlord.
I've nothing for sale.
I'm buying your station.
You're going to jail.

My fistful of money –
It seems such a shame
When bedtime arrives
And it's only a game.

IT'S DONE THIS WAY

My father's twisting it about.
He says, 'I'll get the darn thing out.'
We try to help him if we can.
He says: 'This problem takes a man.'
His eyebrows knit. He sits, he stands,
This baffling object in his hands.
He twists, he frets, perspires and fumes
While we escape to other rooms.
Then finally, in deep despair,
He slumps defeated in his chair.
My father is an awful boob.
He's failed AGAIN with Rubik's Cube.

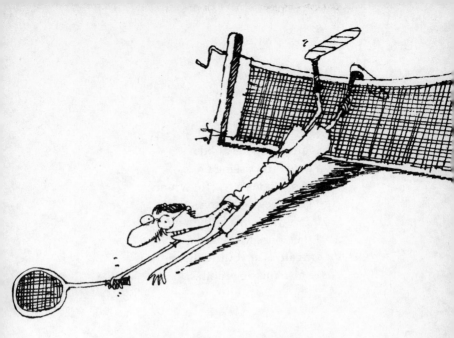

ANYONE FOR TENNIS?

When they shouted, 'Game and set,'
Cousin Henry jumped the net.
He came a thud upon his head
And now plays dominoes instead.

WINDY

The gale upon our holidays
Was not your passing breeze.
It gave our tents a fearful wrench
And bent the frantic trees.
So, if you've seen a flying tent,
And then observe another,
Please call us at your earliest,
We're also missing mother.

THEY'RE AWFUL

I hate them a lot …
People who are always telling the plot
Of television serials,
And how books end,
The menu for dinner,
Whether it's cold or hot;
Who always want to ride in the front seat of cars,
Whether it's their place
Or not
And who are always interrupting
And shouting,
'WHAT?'
I hate the lot.

SOMEWHERE

It's somewhere round the corner
Or so I've heard them say
And everybody wants to go
But no one knows the way.

The days are full of summer
And staying by the sea.
There's apple pie for breakfast
And what you like for tea.

And even running messages
Can be a lot of fun
While washing's not compulsory
And hair can stay undone.

Where chocolates are handy;
Please take another box.
Where only older people
Have mumps or chickenpox.

Where teachers are well hidden
And if you want the truth,
The dentist is forbidden
To touch another tooth.

The people spend their evenings
By walking on their hands
While motorcars are driven
By mostly rubber bands.

And there will be no shrieking
On what a child should do
With parents never speaking
Unless they're spoken to.

With never smell of cartridge
For guns are out of bounds.
Oh happy is the partridge
While foxes chase the hounds.

Where every tree is singing;
Where every bird is free.
With apple pie for breakfast
And what you like for tea.

No television cricket;
No giving up my chair.
I'd like to buy a ticket
If only I knew where.

A moody pterodactyl said,
'I'm fearsome so they tell me.
Though grandly named, I'm so ashamed
That nobody can spell me.'

A Few Scraps

When father does the carving,
It's wiser not to linger.
With any luck he'll carve the duck
But, now and then, a finger.

Little Mary, looking wistful,
Eats her jelly by the fistful.
On the floor it slips and sloshes,
That's why everyone wears goloshes.

Young Arthur has an appetite
You simply can't ignore.
While other people have enough
He always asks for more.
He sets about his eating tasks
And leaves us so unnerved
One question that we NEVER ask
Is, 'Are you being served?'

COUNTRY LUNCH

The basket is a big one, the billycan immense.
We carry them so carefully when getting through the
    fence.
The wind is full of hay smell and hawks patrol the sky.
    When we take the lunches out,
    Jeremy and I.

The harvester is whirring, it cuts the heads of wheat,
The dusty whirlwinds spiralling in columns through
    the heat.
There could be summer snakes about, or so our
    mother said.
    That's why we're walking warily
    And watching where we tread.

We've seen the paddock growing, for magical the rain,
With each stalk putting out its flags and nourishing
    its grain.
We've seen old farmers shaking heads because the
    season's dry;
    And we have been a part of it,
    Jeremy and I.

For country folk are worriers and though it's not a crime,
Yet parents seem (says Jeremy) to do it all the time ...
The bills, the taxes and the kids and how the dams
    are low
        And so it sets us wondering
        Why people worry so.

But then it happens. Storms arrive and creeks go mad
    and flood
And there is gold in every drop and diamonds in
    the mud.
The neighbours call to celebrate, with sausage-rolls
    and tea
        And everything comes right again
        For Jeremy and me.

So now we take the lunches out. It's 'Hurry up,
    you kids'.
Undoing of the luncheon wraps and rattling billy-lids,
With half a dozen messages. You'll need to understand.
        It's hurry, hurry, hurry,
        With people on the land.

The grain trucks for the silo, the agent for the sheep,
'Now you remember, Jeremy. Your brain is half-asleep,
We'll get another drum of fuel. It won't do any harm.'
    It's orders, orders, orders
    When living on a farm.

'The steak and kidney pie is nice. Your mother's quite a
    cook.'
Our father's eyes are wandering with that slow
    farmer's look
That touches crop and heat-hazed land and plainly it
    will tell
    He cares for me and Jeremy
    And loves his earth as well.

We help him with the pannikins and clean the
    crusty plate.
The crop is ripe for harvesting. Tonight he's
    working late.
The summer's full of wonder (and steak and kidney pie)
    When we take the lunch things home
    Jeremy and I.

Just ...

JUST WHEN ...

It's always the same.
Just when you're playing a game;
Just when it's exciting
And interesting
With everyone racing
And chasing,
Just when you're having so much fun,
Somebody always wants something done!

JUST IN CASE ...

When it's nearly my birthday
And so that people won't be upset
Or forget,
I always think it's kinder,
Just as a reminder,
To leave notes on plates,
Hinting at dates.

Most of Me

EARS

Have you thought to give three cheers
For the usefulness of ears?
Ears will often spring surprises
Coming in such different sizes.
Ears are crinkled, even folded.
Ears turn pink when you are scolded.
Ears can have the oddest habits
Standing rather straight on rabbits.
Ears are little tape-recorders
Catching all the family orders.
Words, according to your mother,
Go in one and out the other.
Each side of your head you'll find them.
Don't forget to wash behind them.
Precious little thanks they'll earn you
Hearing things that don't concern you.

Elbows

The elbow has a certain charm
By being halfway up your arm.
Without it you'd be less than able
But never leave it on the table.

LIPSERVICE

Our lips,
Are meant for hisses
And kisses,
Wisecracks
And quips
But mine are mostly
For fish and chips.

HULLO, INSIDE

Physical-education slides
Show us shots of our insides.
Every day I pat my skin,
'Thanks for keeping it all in.'

TAILPIECE

Tongues we use for talking.
Hands we clasp and link.
Feet are meant for walking.
Heads are where we think.
Toes are what we wiggle.
Knees are what we bend.
Then there's what we sit on
And that's about the end.

Also by Wakefield Press

OTHER TIMES

Andrew Male

Andrew Male takes a journey through the life and times of Max Fatchen in this affectionate and surprising biography. Along the way, he reproduces some of Max's best writing, including unpublished treasures.

Wakefield Press has been publishing good Australian books for over fifty years. For a catalogue of current and forthcoming titles, or to add your name to our mailing list, send your name and address to

Wakefield Press, Box 2266,
Kent Town, South Australia 5071.

TELEPHONE (08) 8362 8800 FAX (08) 8362 7592
WEB www.wakefieldpress.com.au

Wakefield Press thanks Wirra Wirra Vineyards and Arts South Australia for their continued support.